Samuel Fᵣ

Dr. Ride's Americ...
Beach House

by Liza Birkenmeier

ıl SAMUEL FRENCH lı

FOR PRODUCTION ENQUIRIES

UNITED STATES AND CANADA
info@concordtheatricals.com
1-866-979-0447

UNITED KINGDOM AND EUROPE
licensing@concordtheatricals.co.uk
020-7054-7200

Each title is subject to availability from Concord Theatricals Corp., depending upon country of performance. Please be aware that *DR. RIDE'S AMERICAN BEACH HOUSE* may not be licensed by Concord Theatricals Corp. in your territory. Professional and amateur producers should contact the nearest Concord Theatricals Corp. office or licensing partner to verify availability.

system, or transmitted in any form, by any means, now known or yet to be invented, including mechanical, electronic, photocopying, recording, videotaping, or otherwise, without the prior written permission of the publisher. No one shall upload this title(s), or part of this title(s), to any social media websites.

For all enquiries regarding motion picture, television, and other media rights, please contact Concord Theatricals Corp.

MUSIC USE NOTE

Licensees are solely responsible for obtaining formal written permission from copyright owners to use copyrighted music in the performance of this play and are strongly cautioned to do so. If no such permission is obtained by the licensee, then the licensee must use only original music that the licensee owns and controls. Licensees are solely responsible and liable for all music clearances and shall indemnify the copyright owners of the play(s) and their licensing agent, Concord Theatricals Corp., against any costs, expenses, losses and liabilities arising from the use of music by licensees. Please contact the appropriate music licensing authority in your territory for the rights to any incidental music.

IMPORTANT BILLING AND CREDIT REQUIREMENTS

If you have obtained performance rights to this title, please refer to your licensing agreement for important billing and credit requirements.

DR. RIDE'S AMERICAN BEACH HOUSE received its world premiere, produced by Ars Nova, at Greenwich House in New York City on November 5, 2019. The performance was directed by Katie Brook, with scenic design by Kimie Nishikawa, costume design by Melissa Ng, lighting design by Oona Curley, and sound design by Ben Williams. The production stage manager was Alex H. Hajjar. The cast was as follows:

HARRIET . . . . Kristen Sieh

MATILDA . . . . Erin Markey

MEG . . . . Marga Gomez

NORMA . . . . Susan Blommaert

CHARACTERS

HARRIET – grumpier than usual, tired of herself
MATILDA – focal point of most parties
MEG – loves metal music because it's a burden to be this smart
NORMA – a martyr for building maintenance
RADIO VOICES – male

SETTING

A roof.
Near Highway 55 and the Mississippi River in South St. Louis, Missouri.

TIME

Friday, June 17, 1983.
(The sun set at 8:27 p.m. CDT in St. Louis, Missouri
and 8:22 p.m. EDT in Cape Canaveral, Florida.)

AUTHOR'S NOTES

When figures perform for each other within the text, they do it boldly and to the fullest extent of their abilities; it's all right for this to be uncomfortable or chaotic.

A slash (/) indicates an interruption, though there could be more interruptions than are noted.

(**HARRIET** *sits on the roof near a 1980 double-cassette radio. She surveys the neighborhood with binoculars.*)

(*A voice from somewhere:*)

MATILDA. (*Offstage.*) Harriet!

(**HARRIET** *calls out:*)

HARRIET. I'm on the roof!

(**MATILDA***'s footsteps up the stairs.*)

MATILDA. (*Offstage.*) I only have forty-five minutes!

(**MATILDA** *appears in a patterned restaurant uniform dress, apron in hand.*)

HARRIET. What took you so long?

MATILDA. Nothing took me anything.

HARRIET. I thought you might have gone home.

MATILDA. For what?

HARRIET. Leslie.

MATILDA. Ugh!

HARRIET. How's she doing?

MATILDA. Horrific. It's a monster poop virus; she's like a leaky Hot Pocket. I talked to Arthur a moment but I –

(*She gestures to the pack of Salem Light cigarettes in* **HARRIET***'s pocket.*)

(**HARRIET** *is caught.*)

What are those?

HARRIET. What. Nothing.

(**MATILDA** *pulls the pack of cigarettes out of* **HARRIET***'s pocket.*)

There's only one left. Last one. Of my life.

(**MATILDA** *takes the last cigarette, lights it, smokes.*)

MATILDA. Look what you're making me do.

(*She passes the cigarette to* **HARRIET**.)

(*They share.*)

HARRIET. This is really the last one of our lives.

(**MATILDA** *enjoys the cigarette – sings or hums something irritatingly upbeat for only a second –*)

Did Arthur say anything?

MATILDA. I thought he'd be begging me to get over there but –

(*She shakes her head.*)

And did I tell you that a door-to-door Mormon assumed Arthur had a more advanced degree than I / do? He –

HARRIET. I mean about. The car.

(*Tiny still.*)

MATILDA. Not yet.

(**HARRIET** *exhales, disappointed.*)

The Mormon said *and what was your husband studying* and I said *wouldn't we all like to know.* I gave him a suggested reading list.

HARRIET. Why did you open the door?

MATILDA. I sincerely want someone to kidnap me.

HARRIET. You make / me so nervous.

MATILDA. So he did believe, after a minute he believed I was smarter than Arthur because I told him I was. But that was the biggest conversion that could happen.

---

*A license to produce *Dr. Ride's American Beach House* does not include a performance license for any third-party or copyrighted music. Licensees should create an original composition or use music in the public domain. For further information, please see Music Use Note on page 3.

I stood at the door and let him ask me about Jesus, but I thought – I said: You're going to have to offer something more inspiring if you want to tempt me out of my existence. He gave up quickly.

HARRIET. Good.

MATILDA. And then he turned around and we both saw this crushed-up – this little knotted *thing* on the steps that looked like a bright, a shiny – a red plant. I said: What is that. He looked at it and made this stupid distraught face and I looked closer and it. It was this balled-up – these organs. Mammal…guts. A little, some – ugh – a squirrel's insides that had been pulled out by something, or – it was disgusting. And he looked back at me and I said: Pick that up. And he said what and I said get that off of my steps. And he did. And so I was glad he came over.

HARRIET. You'd better take Leslie to the doctor.

MATILDA. Have your own kid. Just kidding. Don't.

HARRIET. You'll be convicted of child neglect. You'll be sentenced to the electric chair. I'll have to dissolve the Book Club and / take up needlepointing.

MATILDA. Right after that was the first time – the first time in years – I'd felt like writing a poem about something.

HARRIET. Good.

MATILDA. I was sure you'd be more excited about that.

HARRIET. I'm excited.

> (**MATILDA** *sings whatever she had started singing.**)
>
> (*She makes* **HARRIET** *join* –)
>
> (*Suddenly:*)

MATILDA. I invited Meg.

---

*A license to produce *Dr. Ride's American Beach House* does not include a performance license for any third-party or copyrighted music. Licensees should create an original composition or use music in the public domain. For further information, please see Music Use Note on page 3.

HARRIET. *(Devastated.)* Why? Who?

MATILDA. I thought you wanted me to!

HARRIET. Why would I want you to do that? I don't know who that is.

MATILDA. Do you have any beer?

HARRIET. I thought you were going to pick it up on the way, but.

MATILDA. I was distracted / by my call to –

HARRIET. I thought you came directly from work.

MATILDA. I only – I did!

> (**HARRIET** *sighs.*)

HARRIET. I have some here.

MATILDA. Why are you mad at everything I say?

HARRIET. I'm. Hungry.

MATILDA. Well you only ate about thirty raviolis at work.

HARRIET. Never say ravioli.

> *(She stands. Stubs out her cigarette?)*

I thought you'd know about the car by now.

MATILDA. Sorry.

> (**HARRIET** *disappears downstairs.*)
>
> (**MATILDA** *takes the binoculars. She examines them but doesn't look through them.*)
>
> *(She turns on the radio...a low voice, the news – probably inaudible to the audience.)*
>
> (**HARRIET** *comes back up with two beers and a pint of ice cream. She pops both of the beers open.*)

HARRIET. Here you go, princess.

MATILDA. Thank you.

> (**HARRIET** *hands* **MATILDA** *the can or bottle –)*
>
> (**MATILDA** *drinks, walks to the edge of the roof with the binoculars, looks at the neighbors – or whatever's out there.*)

(**HARRIET** *sits and stabs the too-frozen ice cream with a spoon.*)

HARRIET. I thought the attractive people might be back and. And I / could –

MATILDA. *(Re: binoculars.)* Good idea.

HARRIET. I thought I might be able to look into their kitchen and see what they cook for dinner. Do you think they're serial killers?

MATILDA. Their place is nice.

HARRIET. Where did they go? Can you see the Riverboat McDonald's?

MATILDA. Ick, no.

HARRIET. I don't care for that aesthetic. Mark Twain, et cetera.

MATILDA. They're probably photographers for National Geographic...and they went to Reykjavík to take pictures of the Aurora Borealis or a plague or – an animal plague.

HARRIET. The vagaries of their home life are the reasons I wake up.

MATILDA. *(Re: the radio.)* What were they saying?

HARRIET. They're starting the countdown I guess.

MATILDA. What do they count back from, nine million?

(**HARRIET** *shrugs. She finally – violently – retrieves a spoonful of ice cream.*)

(**MATILDA** *takes the binoculars away from her face.*)

Are you pregnant or something?

HARRIET. Why would you be disgusting?

MATILDA. Are you calling procreation with Luke disgusting?

HARRIET. Carbon refigured into fetal cells is disgusting, and sex with Luke is disgusting too, yes, now that you mention it.

(**MATILDA** *approaches* **HARRIET**, *straddles her legs or sits in her lap.*)

(She puts her face extremely close to **HARRIET***'s.)*

*(***HARRIET*** turns off the radio.)*

HARRIET. Who *is* Meg?

MATILDA. You know her.

HARRIET. I don't. I really. Do not know her.

MATILDA. You've seen her. I love her. She works across the street.

HARRIET. At the laundry?

MATILDA. No, at City Hospital. The front part of the – right there – directly across / the street.

HARRIET. How do you know her?

MATILDA. From walking across the goddamn street.

HARRIET. I don't understand you.

MATILDA. And no one ever will.

HARRIET. I thought this was a *sacred* – / a –

MATILDA. A what? You said – two weeks ago you said – you were worried about the future of the Two Serious Ladies Book Club! I only wanted to *help* –

*(***HARRIET*** puts her head into* **MATILDA***'s chest.)*

I think you miss Luke, cupcake.

HARRIET. *(Muffled.)* I don't.

MATILDA. Our problem was that we weren't interested enough in cocaine in graduate school. If we had been more eccentric or or or *high*, people would be asking us about our inspiration by now. Like Leroy.

HARRIET. Never say Leroy. Never talk about men on / the roof.

MATILDA. Remember his poem called Shrapnel?

HARRIET. Was it / really called Shrapnel?

MATILDA. *(An Irish brogue recitation.)* Oh the barracks, oh war bombs war bombs. I am a man; my hand – it bleeds blood...!

(She sings emphatically with her bad Irish brogue:)

H, A, DOUBLE R, I,
G, A, N SPELLS HARRIGAN.
PROUD OF ALL THE IRISH BLOOD WITHIN ME;
DIVIL A MAN CAN SAY A WORD AGIN ME.
H, A, DOUBLE R, I,
G, A, N, YOU SEE...
IS A NAME THAT A SHAME / NEVER HAS

HARRIET. Our problem is that we're in Missouri.

MATILDA. Our problem is that we never got away from nuns.

HARRIET. Our problem is – yes – and / now we –

MATILDA. Our problem is that we had unrealistic expectations because we never got anyone else's opinions.

HARRIET. *(Muffled.)* Our problem is that we're bad at writing.

> (**MATILDA** *pulls back from* **HARRIET***, truly offended. She holds* **HARRIET***'s face.)*

MATILDA. Speak for yourself.

HARRIET. You're brilliant.

MATILDA. Do you remember the time you ate a piece of chalk?

HARRIET. *I thought it was a mint.*

MATILDA. It didn't give you a clue that it was sitting underneath a dartboard...

HARRIET. Never talk / about this again.

MATILDA. In a *bucket*? I'll never forget how your teeth looked. How your / mouth was –

HARRIET. I only tried to have a friend who wasn't you for one week.

MATILDA. It was the funniest thing that has ever happened to anybody I've ever met.

HARRIET. Were you always horrible?

MATILDA. Yes.

HARRIET. I hate it when you bring that up. That still really embarrasses / me.

MATILDA. I meant – all I meant was that yes. If one of us is brilliant, maybe it's not you.

*(She looks at **HARRIET** through the binoculars. She steps as far away as she can so that she can properly see.)*

HARRIET. Don't look at me.

*(**MATILDA** keeps looking.)*

MATILDA. Why do you keep making that face / you make –

HARRIET. What?

MATILDA. – when you pet dogs?

HARRIET. I'm not!

MATILDA. You look like you're…in pain. But really you feel passion for a second and you don't like it.

*(**HARRIET** turns the radio up. News about Sally Ride.)*

What time do they go?

HARRIET. The morning.

(She listens. A commercial becomes audible.)*

MATILDA. I don't understand the point if there are no extraterrestrials that we want to do chemistry tricks with or, / or, or that we can –

HARRIET. Domesticate. Alien pets.

MATILDA. Or that can – save us! What are they trying to get?

HARRIET. They wave at Russia I think.

MATILDA. And then what does Russia do? *(Figuring out Russian accent.)* Hello. *Hello.* Hello!

HARRIET. Hello – Yuri?

MATILDA. Ronald? Reagan? Hello?

HARRIET. Hi.

MATILDA. Ronald!

HARRIET. I pray for you in your totalitarian darkness.

MATILDA. / Thank you.

---

*A license to produce *Dr. Ride's American Beach House* does not include a performance license for any third-party or copyrighted recordings. Licensees should create their own.

HARRIET. Goodnight, Yuri.

MATILDA. Sleep tight.

HARRIET. Goodnight.

MATILDA. Goodnight.

HARRIET. Goodnight.

MATILDA. Goodnight.

> *(Maybe they call out a few more times – testing how loud they can be –)*
>
> *(**MATILDA** doesn't want this to end...)*
>
> *(Finally, **HARRIET** sighs, heavily.)*

HARRIET. Okay we have to stop talking about men.

> *(Somewhere –)*
>
> *(Banging, doors, commotion –)*
>
> *(A voice from below:)*

NORMA. *(Offstage.)* HARRIET!

HARRIET. I'm on the roof!

> *(**HARRIET** and **MATILDA** go to the edge of the roof, peer over – onto the street.)*
>
> *(They yell back and forth to **NORMA**, below:)*

NORMA. *(Offstage.)* I might need your help closing this.

> *(**HARRIET** thinks to complete **NORMA**'s sentence. Doesn't.)*

(Offstage.) Trunk.

MATILDA. Hi, Norma.

NORMA. *(Offstage, unhappy.)* Hi.

HARRIET. Want a beer?

NORMA. *(Offstage.)* Ah? No thank. You. Whad'a –. What are you doing up there?

HARRIET. Listening to the radio.

NORMA. *(Offstage.)* Are you...

> *(She is dancing, but this is invisible.)*

HARRIET. I wanted to hear Sally Ride say bye.

NORMA. *(Offstage.)* What?

HARRIET. I want to hear Sally Ride. Say *bye*.

NORMA. *(Offstage.)* What?

HARRIET. To. Earth.

NORMA. *(Offstage.)* What?

HARRIET. The astronauts.

NORMA. *(Offstage.)* I'll be d'ed if they send more caca up to space before they can make...something...

HARRIET. What?

NORMA. *(Offstage.)* ...useful.

HARRIET. Well someone thinks it's useful. Because of Russia I guess.

NORMA. *(Offstage.)* Why'd we got to show them our diddlywhackers?

MATILDA. Careful, Harriet just made a rule about – we're / not discussing –

HARRIET. Did you end up finding the right sprocket?

> (**NORMA** *grunts – a couple of bangs. She's trying to close the trunk?*)

NORMA. *(Offstage.)* Ah. My sister helped. We went to the Hardware. Store. But now I can't get this gosh d'ed –

HARRIET. Where is she?

NORMA. *(Offstage.)* Ah. What?

HARRIET. Where's Lucille?

> (**NORMA** *grunts and sighs – greater frustration – she's [still] trying to slam the truck? Where's her sister?*)

Want me to come down?

NORMA. *(Offstage.)* No she's. Putting the groceries in the. LUCILLE! LUCILLE! LUCILLE! LUCILLE! LUCILLE! LUCILLE! Oh she.

> *(A door opens. Movement –)*
>
> *(The sound of a trunk shutting.)*

She did it.

*(They watch **NORMA** go inside – a door slams.)*

HARRIET. She's mad at me since I went out of town. She's – she's like my – like someone's –

MATILDA. I brought you a present.

HARRIET. What.

MATILDA. What do you think it is?

HARRIET. I hope it's not something you're going to make me read.

MATILDA. *(Surprised.)* Why not?

HARRIET. I used to be smarter than you but something happened.

MATILDA. All right: we all know you were a better / *student,* which...

HARRIET. I was complimenting you!

MATILDA. No you / weren't.

HARRIET. I – / *yes.*

MATILDA. Do you want your present or not?!

HARRIET. I want it.

MATILDA. You want it...a lot?

HARRIET. I really want it.

MATILDA. Even if it's something you have to read?

HARRIET. I fucking want it.

MATILDA. Oh you do?

HARRIET. I do!

MATILDA. How bad do you want it?

> *(**HARRIET** sighs – maybe this is funny?)*
>
> *(Maybe not.)*

HARRIET. I really, really, really, really, really...

MATILDA. All right. It's a Sally Ride Going Away Present.

HARRIET. You are very nice.

MATILDA. Thank you. I'm very nurturing, and very nice.

> *(She goes to her folded-up apron – [Or a bag? Or something?])*

(The present isn't there. She panics a moment.
She looks down the stairs, or even leaves for a
second – did she drop it?)

MATILDA. Shit.

HARRIET. You lost it?

MATILDA. I dropped it. It was reading material anyway. I was going to make you read something anyway.

HARRIET. I'm still annoyed from when you made me read *Silkworm*, I mean *Nightworm*, I / mean *Nightwood*.

MATILDA. I got you the – it was the Sally Ride Time Magazine. With the cover and that article.

HARRIET. I have it.

MATILDA. You said you wanted it.

HARRIET. So I got it.

MATILDA. You didn't say.

HARRIET. Well it's fine that you lost it then, isn't it.

MATILDA. Ugh! You remind me of my uncle that I hate.

HARRIET. Did you read it?

MATILDA. Not the whole thing. I picked it up on the way here and tried to read it in the Sinclair parking lot, but it was long.

HARRIET. It's good.

MATILDA. It is good. It's weird that she played tennis.

HARRIET. Why is that weird?

MATILDA. It's too many skills.

HARRIET. She has every skill. She has infinite / skills.

MATILDA. You're like Molly Tyson.

HARRIET. *(Very disappointed.)* What?

MATILDA. The college friend who likes Shakespeare. / Molly Tyson.

HARRIET. I know who Molly Tyson is.

MATILDA. Yes! What? That part was adorable! It made me think that you were like Molly Tyson and I was like Sally Ride.

HARRIET. *Why?* What do you think about yourself? Do you think of yourself as a physicist? / How do you *see* yourself –

MATILDA. A'righta'righta'right you can be whomever you want to be, pookie.

HARRIET. I'm Sally Ride and *you're* / Molly Tyson.

MATILDA. We're always idiots, and we always do this. No one's even one person anyway.

HARRIET. I'm *much* more –. What – what? Everyone's one person.

MATILDA. Everyone's many people.

HARRIET. I hate it when you have philosophies.

MATILDA. / I don't have philosophies, I have truths.

> (**NORMA** *climbs out of the window.*)

NORMA. I. Now the other. Thing'ta do is I need you to move that air conditioning unit. You left it running. When you left. /'Town.

HARRIET. I know.

NORMA. I heard a *drip drip*.

HARRIET. Uh-huh.

NORMA. And I think *am I loony?* But there's. Definitely a drip. I'm thinking *oh no*. What's busted?

HARRIET. I left it on.

NORMA. After a few hours, *drip drip*. Then I see what – water. On the walk, and I think: dagnabbit because I. Care about safety.

HARRIET. That's right.

NORMA. We got kids coming in for tours. / Can't have.

MATILDA. / You do?

HARRIET. I'll make sure I turn it off when I can.

NORMA. Well. No. The problem is we're gonna have to find a. Different window. Can't be dripping over the. See this?

> (*She goes to the edge.* **HARRIET** *is nervous about how close* **NORMA** *is to the edge, maybe takes*

her arm or something. **NORMA** *points down to the street.)*

HARRIET. Yeah.

NORMA. See this?

HARRIET. Yeah.

NORMA. Can't.

HARRIET. Yeah.

NORMA. Have this on the walk like this.

HARRIET. All right.

NORMA. So I was hoping you could come down. And move it.

HARRIET. All right.

NORMA. I care about safety and I care about money. And someone's gonna fine the. If someone. So if you could do that pretty. Much now. I'd sure appreciate it.

HARRIET. In a few minutes. Matilda can help me. / We'll move it.

MATILDA. I can?

NORMA. I better get in to Lucille. She doesn't like. You. She doesn't like either one of you.

> *(Quiet.)*

She's probably already busted into those Hawaiian rolls. She's like a vacuum. Sometimes I look at her and say *wah'yah must really like. To eat.* But it doesn't seem to insult her.

> *(They watch* **NORMA** *go inside.)*
>
> *(A door shuts.)*
>
> *(They're quiet.)*

MATILDA. Are you thinking about your mom?

> *(***HARRIET*** *shrugs.)*

We don't have to talk about it, cupcake.

> *(***HARRIET*** *looks out of the binoculars.)*
>
> *(She keeps looking through them as she speaks. She might look through them the entire time she tells this part of the story:)*

HARRIET. I met a man?

MATILDA. What?

HARRIET. I don't want to break the rule, but let's talk about this through my perspective. He is an object and I am the subject. He is the, the, *commodity* and I'm the –

MATILDA. Of course.

HARRIET. I was at the hospice center.

MATILDA. Ick.

HARRIET. I was getting into the elevator and this man comes in after me, and he says *you were really moving fast there*. And I say *oh*. Because I didn't think I was moving fast, because I was limping. And he said that maybe he didn't notice I was limping because / he was *also* limping.

MATILDA. Why were you limping. Why were you limping.

HARRIET. My shoe was broken. And then we got out of the elevator.

MATILDA. Okay.

HARRIET. And then the next day, I was in the hallway and I saw him. He was limping down. And he said: well, looks like we should get lunch. And I said sure.

MATILDA. Poor Luke's gonna jump / off a cliff.

HARRIET. Okay, no, no. So at first: so. He shows me his motorcycle and of course I'm –

(*She waves her hand, desultory, wrist limp.*)

MATILDA. I don't know what that means.

HARRIET. I don't know.

MATILDA. You don't know about the entire idea of motor / cycles, or –

HARRIET. I don't know, I don't know. We go into the cafeteria.

MATILDA. It's like a hospital cafeteria?

HARRIET. Yes.

MATILDA. What did you eat?

HARRIET. Jell-O.

MATILDA. What kind.

HARRIET. Orange.

MATILDA. Uck.

HARRIET. It was the kind they had. It had canned whipped cream on top.

MATILDA. Why are you disgusting?

HARRIET. I loved it.

MATILDA. Uck. What did he eat?

HARRIET. Some big – pile of – I'm not sure. Meat. And he tells me that he is having trouble getting a girlfriend.

MATILDA. Is that why he's at the hospice center? To find a girlfriend?

HARRIET. His father was dying, but we didn't talk about it.

MATILDA. How old was he?

HARRIET. The guy or his father?

MATILDA. The guy.

HARRIET. Oh. Forty. Fifty.

MATILDA. Wow. Was he good-looking?

HARRIET. Well isn't that the question. I couldn't *see* him, I couldn't / even tell if –

MATILDA. What do you mean.

HARRIET. He had so much hair on his face. He had so much hair. He had this giant beard like he was out of the bible. I said look, you might be a good-looking guy, but you just have too much hair on your face for me to be able to *know*.

MATILDA. Is that really what you said to him out loud?

HARRIET. Yes! He said he was having trouble getting a girlfriend, and I told him...

(*A car alarm goes off – maybe* **HARRIET** *looks toward the sound with the binoculars.*)

I told him, I said: You have a motorcycle and you collect marbles, what's not to like?

MATILDA. He collects marbles?

HARRIET. Yes! And he laughed and I said: Listen. I cannot see your face. That is the one thing I have to tell you. And he wasn't insulted – he – he laughed!

MATILDA. He was in love.

HARRIET. Well then I told him to take me on a ride on his motorcycle.

MATILDA. No you didn't.

HARRIET. I did.

MATILDA. No.

HARRIET. Truly.

MATILDA. You're yanking / me.

HARRIET. You don't understand what it's like to be me, because every single person who walks into the restaurant is fascinated by you.

MATILDA. I can't help that I'm a Leo.

HARRIET. Well I got a glimpse is all I mean, of what it is to be – you. And I asked him: I / said take me –

MATILDA. You didn't *go* though –

> (**HARRIET** *nods.*)

What happened? You waited three days to tell me this? Are / you deceased?

HARRIET. I've only seen you at work since Leslie's / been sick –

MATILDA. Tell me, tell me, tell me: open your mouth, and tell – wait! Do we need another beer?

HARRIET. We need another beer.

> (*She moves to fetch the beer.*)

MATILDA. No! Let me get it.

> (*She runs downstairs, singing** [probably the same upbeat song she sang earlier].* **HARRIET**

---

*A license to produce *Dr. Ride's American Beach House* does not include a performance license for any third-party or copyrighted music. Licensees should create an original composition or use music in the public domain. For further information, please see Music Use Note on page 3.

sits at the table, puts her head down or into her hands.)

*(**MATILDA** materializes with two more beers. She keeps singing until she sees that **HARRIET** is noticeably distressed.)*

HARRIET. So I say: Well. Take me out on your motorcycle. It was a Harley.

MATILDA. *(Re: **HARRIET**'s expression.)* Hey.

HARRIET. Nothing. It's nothing. And he looks like I tell him he's won the lotto. He pays for our lunch.

MATILDA. Come here.

*(**HARRIET** shakes her head, no. Maybe she is quiet for a long time.)*

Did this person hurt you?

*(**HARRIET** shakes her head.)*

Is this about Luke?

*(**HARRIET** shakes her head.)*

Your mom?

(Quiet.)

HARRIET. She's in so much pain.

MATILDA. I'm sorry.

HARRIET. She's in so much pain.

MATILDA. Yeah.

HARRIET. So. Anyway, so he –

(Quiet.)

He was so happy. He is so excited to take me on this thing – which is just – huge. He – and *oh* how stupid but / he...

MATILDA. What. What.

HARRIET. He tells me that the reason he is limping is because of a *motorcycle accident.*

MATILDA. Jesus almighty.

HARRIET. I know. So, I say *what?* And he says he crashed his motorcycle somewhere, he skidded off a highway out by – somewhere – and messed up his whole right side. He ruined his entire bike, he says, so then – he goes out and he gets *another* one. I think: this is a bad sign.

MATILDA. You're killing me, pookie.

HARRIET. So this is his *new* motorcycle and I say: Have you murdered anyone on this thing before? And he laughs? But I hop on anyway, and we –

(She gestures: go.)

MATILDA. You weren't scared?

HARRIET. No. So we go. And. It's really something. We go by the ocean, and I'm so – I'm – I felt like I could do anything.

MATILDA. Did you tell him you had a boyfriend?

HARRIET. And at one point all this sand was in my hair and face and I didn't mind.

MATILDA. Where did you go?

HARRIET. I'm going to tell you, but –

MATILDA. No!

HARRIET. You can't have any opinions.

MATILDA. Say it I will die say it.

*(**HARRIET** covers **MATILDA**'s mouth.)*

HARRIET. I went to his house.

MATILDA. This is / horrible.

HARRIET. Shh. I know! What came over me? But I go right on into his house, where he has taxidermy stuff on the walls.

MATILDA. Uh-oh.

HARRIET. Alligators. It's got this one orange sofa in the living room, but nothing else – except the dead stuff, and then the carpet is light blue, a sort of – something that should never be on a floor. I said to him *your house* *is the opposite of the earth* and he said *what?* And I said *never mind.*

MATILDA. Uh-huh.

HARRIET. We go upstairs. It's a weird house – the roof's like this –

> *(She tilts her hand, a sharp angle down.)*

And we go – I feel almost embarrassed!

MATILDA. Why? Why?

HARRIET. He opens the door to his room, and I just take off all my clothes.

MATILDA. No!

HARRIET. Matilda! I'm telling you: for once in my – I was only. I have never had more control of a room, a. I could have told this person to stab his own mother. I could have –. I was imbued with this *power.* Maybe other people have had this before, but – I haven't.

MATILDA. You took off all of your clothes. What did you *say?*

HARRIET. Nothing! I took them all off. I put them on the bed. I sat there naked. He just looked at me. He closed the blinds. The room was small, and the house was very close to the house next door. He turned on the radio, and it was Loretta Lynn – Coal Miner's Daughter. So I was sitting there – we were quiet for a / minute –

> *(**MATILDA** interrupts – hums or sings – impersonating Loretta Lynn [well]...*)*
>
> *(She stops when **HARRIET** speaks.)*

And then. It became too overwhelming. He kept sitting there. Like a pet in a leather jacket.

MATILDA. Did you want him to touch you?

HARRIET. I said *you can touch me.*

MATILDA. You did?

---

*A license to produce *Dr. Ride's American Beach House* does not include a performance license for any third-party or copyrighted music. Licensees should create an original composition or use music in the public domain. For further information, please see Music Use Note on page 3.

HARRIET. He was waiting for permission, I knew. I said *go ahead. Touch me.*

MATILDA. And he did?

HARRIET. He did. He put his hand right here.

(She puts her hand on her inner thigh.)

And I said *no.* I said *touch me here.*

(She puts her hand on her neck.)

*(**MATILDA** gasps as if this is somehow more lascivious. Maybe she mirrors **HARRIET**.)*

And he held his hand there, and I said *put your hand on my face* and he did. And I then I said *put your hand on my arm, put your hand on my knee, put your other hand here, your other hand here, your other hand here, your other hand here.* All over. And then I said stop. And I said *lie down,* and he did, and now the radio was playing a song I never heard before. Not a good one. It was still country music – something about – it had *talking* in it. Some man's voice started saying: *This is a song about a car accident.* It was awful.

MATILDA. Did you say anything? About the talking – the country song with talking?

HARRIET. No. I took off his clothes and I said *don't move.* I put my mouth all over his body, really slowly, like I was an alien, like I had never touched skin before. I wasn't trying to be sweet to him. I really only wanted to touch my mouth, my lips to every part of his skin like he was some object that I had to discover. I took my time. I kept getting distracted by that awful song. It was about two children who get killed by a car. I was saying in my own brain: *Stop thinking of dead children. Think of his penis. Think of anything.* And then I was thinking of my dying mother and I kept saying to myself: *Think of anything. Think about his cells, his skin cells. Think about every hair on his whole body.* I owned them all. They were mine and I could have them.

MATILDA. Wow.

HARRIET. And then the song changed, finally, and I was so relieved, and I sat up, and I took his wrists –

(She takes **MATILDA** *by the wrists.)*

And he said: *What do you want to do?* Because he knew. He knew that I could do anything in the entire world. I could have caused a famine.

MATILDA. I wish I had seen you.

HARRIET. And I said *I want to see your face.* And he said *okay* and I took him to the bathroom, and I sat on the edge of the bathtub, and he cut off his beard with scissors and he shaved his face, right there. He got his hair all over everything. And then I could see him.

MATILDA. Jesus, is this a twist? Was his / face deformed?

HARRIET. A little. No. No. Oh, not – his face, I mean – no. It was a face. It was nice. But it changed everything. I didn't care anymore. I didn't want to have power anymore. I was so tired of him all of the sudden.

MATILDA. He made it too easy?

HARRIET. Maybe that's it? I said that he should shower, get – all of the little hairs off, all these hairs stuck to his body – and he did; I watched him. And he dried off, and I looked at every little bit of – all the skin I had touched with my mouth, and it suddenly seemed inanimate. And I'd lost interest in him so I felt.

MATILDA. Annoyed.

HARRIET. I got frightened as soon as he went back to his bed. I felt like I would have to move in with him and live in his bathroom forever because I forgot any way of getting out of there, of getting back home.

MATILDA. I'm glad you're not in his / bathroom anymore.

HARRIET. But I did – yes – I did get out of the bathroom. I went back to his bed and his bare face was so strange. He was happy, so I felt like he was all right, so I felt like I had taken care of him. I remembered I was in control completely – in control. I pulled the covers over us and I said *is it ok if we do this now?* He was helpless, and I liked it, and my face got so hot. My eyes got watery and my mouth did, like I was going to eat the best sandwich on earth – I was excited, which – I have never in my life felt excited to have sex before. *Never.* The – I have never anticipated sex in my entire life in a way that was remotely positive. And I feel a whole new power, like a person who can barbecue, and I think to myself *stop thinking of dying people*, which only makes me think more – and I think to myself *think of how strong you are*, and I manage to get on top of him, I – I – you wouldn't believe what I was like. I had sex with him like he owed it to me. And it felt so good but I kept having to tell myself *you are an organism*, and I kept having to tell myself: *Tie your body down to – think about this music, think about sensations, pleasure, blood, think about what you're making him do, think about your eyes, don't think about anyone shriveling up and dying. Think of food, of – think of full and fat things, warm things, power. Think about living – think about skin, think about. Living.*

MATILDA. It worked.

(**HARRIET** *nods.*)

HARRIET. And then I made him come.

MATILDA. Did he make a sound?

(**HARRIET** *nods.*)

Did you feel – were you happy?

HARRIET. I have no idea. I fell asleep. Almost instantly asleep – I remember – my muscles all –

(*She tenses her muscles.*)

And for a little second I could see a scar down his back from his motorcycle accident and it made me feel like: wow. I healed him. I don't know why. But then – sleep like the dead.

MATILDA. Maybe you loved him.

HARRIET. Mm? Then I woke up, and the strangest thing happened.

MATILDA. *Then* the strangest / thing happened?

HARRIET. There was a song that wasn't country – well it was country – it was this country version of that song we – we thought it was *so funny* in choir? The…third grade. Fourth grade. We thought was *hilarious* / when we –

MATILDA. *(Sings [in the style of a country song].)*
HAVE YOU BEEN TO JESUS FOR THE CLEANSIN' POW'R?
ARE YOU WASHED IN THE BLOOD OF THE LAMB?
ARE YOU FLEE-TEE PLA-DAH IN HIS GRACE THIS HOUR?
/ ARE YOU WASHED IN THE BLOOD OF THE LAMB

> *(**HARRIET** thinks this is very funny –)*
> *(She speaks over **MATILDA**.)*

HARRIET. This reminds me of everything!

> *(She sings along. It gets [nearly] raucous?)*

MATILDA & HARRIET.
ARE YOU WASHED IN THE BLOOD
IN THE SOUL-CLEANSING BLOOD OF THE LAMB?
ARE YOUR GARMENTS SPOTLESS? ARE THEY WHITE AS SNOW.
ARE YOU WASHED IN THE BLOOD OF THE LAMB?

MATILDA.
DEE-LA-SA-SABLEE-DAH THAT ARE –

MATILDA & HARRIET.
STAINED WITH SIN!
AND BE WASHED IN THE BLOOD OF THE LAMB!

MATILDA.
THERE'S A BIDDLEBIDDLE IN THE BIM DA BAH

MATILDA & HARRIET.
OH BE WASHED IN THE BLOOD OF THE LAMB!
ARE YOU WASHED IN THE BLOOD
IN THE SOUL-CLEANSING / BLOOD OF THE

> *(A voice from somewhere:)*

MEG. *(Offstage.)* Hello?

MATILDA. We're on the roof.

> *(She continues to sing, quietly – **HARRIET** is annoyed.)*

(**MEG** *materializes with a bottle of wine and a button-up shirt, maybe even a lab coat?*)

(**MATILDA** *and* **HARRIET** *are surprised to be in awe of her.*)

MEG. Hi.

MATILDA. Hey. Glad you could come.

HARRIET. I'm Harriet.

MEG. I know. I brought this. I felt strange not having read the book so I thought I'd bring...

(*She shrugs, holds out the wine.*)

MATILDA. Oh! I forgot to / tell you.

HARRIET. It's not a real book club.

MEG. Oh! It's. Oh.

HARRIET. Sorry to be disappointing.

MEG. It's just. No, I didn't. / Know.

HARRIET. We're disappointments.

MATILDA. Sorry.

MEG. What kind of club. Is it.

HARRIET. It was a book club until one of the founding members noticed she didn't like reading.

MATILDA. I love reading! You're the one who won't take / my...

HARRIET. I didn't make this up. I think your words were – precisely – *I prefer television.*

MEG. I love reading.

MATILDA. WE ALL LOVE READING. We all love reading. WE LOVE BOOKS. Come'on...in! The Two Serious Ladies Book Club was a fantasy of starting a cultural life in this town –

HARRIET. That died. But it has given / us a reason –

MATILDA. It's given us a *lot.* For example. We say on Fridays to anyone who asks that we are going to the Two Serious Ladies Book Club, and it sounds / more respectable –

HARRIET. No one – no one asks.

MATILDA. Except our husbands.

HARRIET. I don't have a husband.

MATILDA. You have a. You have something.

HARRIET. Do you have a husband?

MEG. Of course not.

> *(Quiet.)*

HARRIET. It's a good reason...for a beer before dark, anyway.

MATILDA. Right! Yes! Can I get you a beer!

MEG. No thank you.

MATILDA. Okay we'll try to be thrilling.

HARRIET. Matilda's thrilling. I'm...

MEG. *(To* **HARRIET.***)* Who is your person? The – your not-husband.

HARRIET. Oh, only a. Graduate student.

> **(MEG** *nods.)*

MEG. Does he or she – this person – where are they?

> **(HARRIET** *stares.)*

HARRIET. No one. Nowhere.

> **(MATILDA** *is utterly baffled by this, maybe hurt.)*

MEG. Have you been – *(Points to the binoculars.)*

HARRIET. I was spying on the people who live over there.

MEG. Do you write about them?

HARRIET. I – no.

MEG. Matilda told me – you –

MATILDA. I told her you were a poet.

HARRIET. So is Matilda.

MEG. I wrote a poem once that was pretty good but I was eight.

> *(Small still.)*

HARRIET. I'm quitting anyway.

MATILDA. Stop.

HARRIET. In my mind, I planned to go away for the weekend – *if* –

(She glares at MATILDA *–)*

If Arthur lets us borrow the car. Come / back and.

MEG. Where would you go?

HARRIET. Quit De Luca's. Quit writing. Move out of this place.

MEG. You live in there?

HARRIET. It's the right setting for Two Serious Ladies Book Club, isn't it?

MEG. What is it.

HARRIET. The Ivan Brock House. It was built by Ivan Brock.

MEG. Who's Ivan Brock?

MATILDA & HARRIET. A poet.

HARRIET. A riverboat poet. He had a riverboat aesthetic. He built it in 1920-something, or *someone* built –

(She shrugs, gestures out.)

But. So I –

MEG. Seemed kinda cool in there.

*(*HARRIET *nods.)*

HARRIET. I thought it would be cool. I thought it would be great. I help the – Norma – she runs it. I help her around the library. I thought: I'll live here and write poems like Ivan Brock. But my sadder reality is that I come out with my chair and table and look out and I am not inspired by this river.

MEG. Was Ivan Brock inspired by the river?

*(*HARRIET *nods, sighs.)*

HARRIET. And I'm retiring.

MATILDA. Ugh I'm exhausted from hearing you announce this every three months.

HARRIET. I just became a new person! I don't want to *wonder* about every –. It isn't romantic to me. It turns out I hate Ivan Brock's poems and more importantly, I'm tired of. Never mind.

MATILDA. Tired of.

*(*HARRIET *looks at* MATILDA *– pointed.)*

(Maybe, suddenly, the sound of crickets is noticeable.)

HARRIET. Everything. And I'm tired of poetry for regular reasons. The same reasons everyone else is.

MATILDA. Ugh shut up and give me / a break.

MEG. Hey, have – sorry – have you got a glass for this? *(The wine.)*

HARRIET. Oh. Yes. Let me get it.

MEG. Oh no no I'll get it.

HARRIET. I'll get it.

MEG. Really, I didn't mean for you –

HARRIET. It's fine.

(She leaves.)

MEG. Can I –? *(The binoculars.)*

MATILDA. Yeah.

*(**MEG** looks at the neighbors.)*

(Or whatever's out there.)

Did you have a better party to go to?

MEG. No.

MATILDA. Sometimes we're more agreeable.

MEG. I'm not uncomfortable.

(Quiet.)

Are you two very serious?

MATILDA. Are we. No – we're – what do you mean?

MEG. The Two Serious Ladies.

MATILDA. Oh oh it's. Oh: *Two Serious Ladies*; it's a book. We read it in graduate school. At the time we felt we deeply related to it but I – we. That was when we had aspirations.

MEG. There's a man trying to kill a bug. Wow. He looks so stupid.

*(**HARRIET** returns with a glass and a book.)*

HARRIET. Sorry I only have these old jam jars.

MEG. That's perfect.

HARRIET. And I brought up this book – the most famous one – of Brock's poems, in case you want to learn about a – about a snail on a bluff.

(**MEG** *keeps looking through the binoculars.*)

Something good out there?

MEG. A man trying to kill a bug. He's terrible. It's in his bed. Oh. He's got it.

(**HARRIET** *and* **MATILDA** *try to see –*)

Oh! It's not! It's not dead! It's on the wall. Oh no it's flying – what is it?

HARRIET. I hope it's not a bee.

MEG. It landed on him.

MATILDA. Ugh.

MEG. Maybe it's just a fly. He doesn't seem frightened. He – no he's flicking it off –

MATILDA. With his bare hands?

MEG. He's got a magazine, or a, or – I don't know.

MATILDA. This is making me itch.

MEG. I want him to kill it.

MATILDA. Is he naked?

MEG. He's awful. He really can't get it. No he's in his work pants and.

HARRIET. Odd.

MEG. Yeah. Do we all look stupid?

(*Quiet.*)

Oh. Oh. He's got it – he's! He's got it. It's dead.

(*She puts the binoculars down and pours herself a huge glass of wine. She opens the book of poems. Flips through.*)

(*She drinks a lot of her wine.*)

(*Toward the poems.*) Ah – this one's kinda funny. This one's about – oh – (*Disappointed.*) Oh. I thought it was

about sex. But I think it's. *(She reads –) O her glassy eyes shock'd o her wild crown tame-èd for –*
I think it's about a deer.

HARRIET. It makes me think that all art is for idiots, and then I get / so sad.

MEG. Aren't there poems you like? Who's – do you have a favorite poet?

HARRIET. / I don't know.

MATILDA. Dr. Seuss.

HARRIET. *("Privately" to* **MATILDA.***)* It really bothers me / when you say that.

MEG. Do you like – sorry do you like – Emily Dickinson or something?

> *(***HARRIET*** *is caught – maybe she clenches her jaw. Maybe she won't let on.)*
>
> *(***MATILDA*** *considers speaking for her – doesn't.)*

HARRIET. Yes.

> *(***MEG*** *nods.)*

MEG. I. Anyway. I would also like to quit my job.

HARRIET. But don't you do something meaningful?

> *(***MEG*** *laughs at* ***HARRIET.***)*

What.

MEG. No, I. I don't know.

HARRIET. How did you get your job?

MEG. Nursing school.

HARRIET. Should I do that?

MEG. No.

MATILDA. *(To* **HARRIET.***)* You'd hate nursing school, cupcake.

HARRIET. What's to hate? I'm fine with studying.

MEG. All of it – studying – nursing school – the hospital, all of it – men. It makes me homicidal.

HARRIET. Toward your patients?

MEG. No. No. Just toward Dr. Dale, a maniac who does night rounds on Thursdays.

HARRIET. Do you / hate men?

MATILDA. What did Dale do?

MEG. It doesn't matter. I go to a psychoanalyst. And no no, I don't hate men; they only make me homicidal. I'll be fine.

MATILDA. Are you / sure?

MEG. All I meant was that nothing means anything. My job. / Medicine.

MATILDA. *(Maybe hardly audible.)* / I do not like them on a spoon,

I do not like them on the moon,

I do not like them...

HARRIET. But it's definite. It's more definite.

MEG. My job?

HARRIET. Yes. I think. Yes. I want. I want everything to be more definite.

MEG. My job isn't more definite. It's barbaric sometimes.

HARRIET. But you have skills.

MEG. Yeah. / I guess.

HARRIET. You have to know about science. Science...is objective –

MEG. Not / really.

MATILDA. No it's not.

MEG. It's from human observation. Poetry is more expressive, but it's. Also human observation.

MATILDA. Perspective.

MEG. Everything has a perspective. Everyone loves pretending that this one thing's a fact and this other thing is an opinion but that's all really mixed up, I think.

HARRIET. Even a medical chart?

MEG. Sure, no, the chart's – a chart. But there's no one person who can look at it and say: this is the absolute truth about what's here. I can look at a patient on our floor and think: this person's gonna get transferred to the unit before lunch. And I know that because of lactate and oxygen levels and on and on like that, but also just looking at a guy and knowing he's going to tank. There aren't a lot of facts. There might not be any plain facts. It's all a mix of – it's a mix.

HARRIET. But I think I want skills.

MEG. I think you want –

HARRIET. What –

MEG. To not have your graduate student anymore.

HARRIET. I don't know why you would assume – why you would assume what I – I don't know / know what I...

MATILDA. You've caught her on a weird day.

HARRIET. On a *weird day*?

MEG. She's right! No – she's right, you're right – Harriet, you're right. I've no idea what you want.

> (*Quiet.*)

But I have an opinion. I think it's cool that you... I think it would be sad if you quit poetry.

HARRIET. / Sure.

MEG. Even if your favorite poet is Emily Dickinson.

HARRIET. She's not –. I don't –. I don't see a problem with Emily Dickinson.

> (**HARRIET** *turns on the radio. Low voices. Something about Sally Ride's departure.*)
>
> (**HARRIET**, **MEG**, *and* **MATILDA** *sit, rapt. This might go on for a while.* **MEG** *might still be reading the poetry.*)
>
> (**MEG** *takes off her button-up shirt [or lab coat]. Beneath it is a thrash metal t-shirt of some kind, the sleeves cut off. She does something to her hair.*)
>
> (*She gestures at* **HARRIET** *– the cigarettes in her pocket.* **HARRIET** *pulls out the pack, remembers it's empty, shows it to* **MEG** *–*)
>
> (*She realizes that* **MEG** *is completely physically transformed.* **MEG** *smiles at* **HARRIET**.)

MATILDA. Can you imagine being Sally Ride's mother?

MEG. / Dr. Ride.

HARRIET. No.

MATILDA. What?

MEG. Dr. Ride. We all call her Sally Ride – the news and everyone.

MATILDA. Harriet loves Sally Ride.

HARRIET. I love her. I love her. I.

MEG. Why?

HARRIET. I…because she's. *(Really has to consider.)* Going away. Because. The first time I saw her, I thought I – in the newspaper, I thought I – I don't know.

MEG. Don't you think we should call her Dr. Ride? Since she's –

> *(They stare at her, a tiny still –)*

HARRIET. Yes.

MATILDA. Her mother must be happy, is what I mean. If my daughter grew up to – I have a daughter – if she grew up to be a physicist astronaut? I would get a t-shirt airbrushed with her, her giant neon face, and I would wear it everywhere and say: do you see this face, this head with this brain? I made this with my fucking cells, with all the fatty materials I didn't vomit. I made this out of cells *in my womb.* I made this woman and put her in goddamn space.

HARRIET. If she gets there.

MATILDA. *(Toward* **HARRIET.***)* You're irritating. Read my horoscope.

HARRIET. What?

> *(***MATILDA*** gestures to a newspaper beside the radio.)*

MATILDA. Is that today's?

> *(***HARRIET*** nods. She flips toward the back of the* Post-Dispatch. *She reads:)*

HARRIET. Leo: If you must make a choice, choose what is best for others. You might have to act against your own longings. Any parental issues require immediate attention.

MATILDA. Ew what's yours?

HARRIET. I'm not in the mood to tell you.

(She flips through the paper.)

MATILDA. *(To* MEG.*)* What's your sign?

*(*MEG *shrugs.)*

MEG. The charming one.

HARRIET. Look. This one calls her – this one – *Miss Ride.*

(She scans the article –)

MEG. What is she doing *right now*? What do you think she's doing?

MATILDA. Okay... I think she and her mother cooked spaghetti, something easy because she has a lot to think about. And she and her mother talked about their whole lives, and how proud they are of each other? I hope they did. And now she's gone home, and she's with her husband or, and they're trying sex stuff they never have before – ah! I hope / she's having the –

MEG. She's a lesbian.

*(*HARRIET *looks up from the paper.)*

MATILDA. Oh. Well I hope she's having / the time of her –

HARRIET. She's not a lesbian!

MEG. Yes she is.

HARRIET. She's. I don't think she. No. She's married to Stephen Hawley.

*(*MEG *shrugs.)*

MEG. All right sure, I – she is. I'm certain she is.

MATILDA. I – okay – yes but no matter what she, or – I hope she's having the time of her life.

HARRIET. She's not with her mother.

MEG. Where is she?

HARRIET. She's eating barbecue.

MATILDA. How do you know that?

HARRIET. I'll have to. So: I was telling Matilda before you got here about this – enlightening experience – it was –

MATILDA. I'm going to fantasize about it / for *weeks*.

HARRIET. I had a bit of a departure from myself.

MEG. In a nice way?

MATILDA. *Nice?*

HARRIET. Oh – I don't – maybe / nice?

MATILDA. Nice if you're in the mood to be murdered / in another state.

HARRIET. Well but I didn't finish!

MATILDA. Long story / short, she had –

HARRIET. I had a motorcycle ride. And / a – a –

MATILDA. I cannot believe either of us / is alive.

HARRIET. I slept with someone I just met.

MATILDA. She was liberated.

MEG. Congratulations.

HARRIET. / Thank you –

MATILDA. Thank you.

HARRIET. And afterwards, woke up – I woke up and it was late at night – I was – my mother's – *anyway*. I was in Apollo Beach, Florida.

MEG. Oh.

HARRIET. I woke up beside this man who I'd just met, who'd just shaved his beard.

MATILDA. And let's – just – keep this on the roof, as it's a relatively big scandal / for South City.

HARRIET. It's fine. It's fine: I don't *belong* to anyone.

MATILDA. I don't know that everybody would agree / with that.

HARRIET. I don't care. It's – it's: so – anyway, so I wake up in the middle of the night in this stranger's house. He says: Do you want to see my marble collection? But I said no, take me somewhere first. We got back on his Harley.

MEG. Harleys are stupid.

HARRIET. I know. I don't know what I was thinking. I know.

MEG. Maybe you were just really interested in him.

HARRIET. No, I wasn't. We go on his motorcycle – hours – we drive for hours, until we get to the beach. The eeriest – it felt like the end of the planet! We go over this narrow / bridge, right over the.

MATILDA. Uck. / Uck.

MEG. *(To MATILDA.)* What. What.

HARRIET. She doesn't like the word planet.

MATILDA. That whole description – ugh.

MEG. The end of the planet?

MATILDA. I hate that word, and I – yes – I. It seems normal to me that it's entirely creepy to remember you live on a *planet*.

MEG. No that's not normal.

MATILDA. Isn't it? *Planet?* / Ah!

HARRIET. No.

MATILDA. It makes me feel like I'm an animal in a desert, in the, in the *dark* – I'm looking at the moon; I don't have any money; I'm next to a cactus; I'm – spinning – *witlessly* – it's. Uck. The whole thing makes me – I lose my appetite.

MEG. Were you / scared?

MATILDA. Ugh.

HARRIET. No, hungry. We walked way down onto the sand.

MATILDA. I can't believe you weren't murdered.

HARRIET. And he said – *do you know what that is – way over there?* And he pointed out to this thing that looked like a factory, and I said *no*. And he said *that's the Kennedy Space Center.* I nearly fell over. Oh, because at this point, I hadn't realized we'd ridden the motorcycle from the Gulf Coast to the Atlantic Ocean.

MEG. / Oh.

MATILDA. She has no sense of direction.

HARRIET. It's true. So I stood there, and I was – sort of – whatever it was – dumbfounded, and he said. He pointed to this little house and said. *That's the NASA Beach House.* And I asked him *what do you mean* – and he said *well.* He said *it's where the astronauts stay the night before their missions.*

MEG. / No.

MATILDA. Really?

HARRIET. He said *Sally Ride is going to stay in that house on Friday night. They all go and barbecue. They stay right there the night before the launch.*

MATILDA. But you hadn't told him?

HARRIET. I hadn't! I hadn't said a thing about it. I didn't say a thing about it! So, she. So that's where she is right now. Dr. Ride is at a beach house. Eating barbecue.

MEG. Wow.

HARRIET. Maybe it was the best thing. / That ever happened.

MATILDA. *(Quietly, as they speak, a spontaneous opera.)*
FOLLOW YOUR HEART TO
YOUR HOPE TO THE ROAD TO THE SKY...

MEG. Maybe you should write a poem about that.

HARRIET. Or I should be an astronaut.

MEG. I mean maybe that inspires you more than the river.

HARRIET. I don't know what inspires me.

MATILDA. Apparently a Harley Davidson.

MEG. You can really sing.

MATILDA. I played Annie Oakley in high school.

HARRIET. She was astonishing.

MEG. You went to high school together?

MATILDA. Yeah, we did. Catholic stuff. Maybe Ivan Brock would have written better poems if he'd had sex with the motorcycle man.

HARRIET. The rule is to not talk about men on the roof.

MEG. I didn't notice that.

HARRIET. In my story about the motorcycle person, I was the subject and he was the object. He was the commodity and I was the.

MEG. Okay.

HARRIET. Really.

MEG. No, sure, sure. I get it. I had a – maybe similar, I guess, a. I was – I met a person in Soulard a few summers ago, and we talked until this bar closed and we drove way out 44...and we.

> *(Small quiet: is she sure she wants to tell this story?)*

We talked all night; I felt – this is very stupid but – I felt like I never knew anyone better than that. We drove so long and stayed at the Super 8 and went swimming at Johnson's Shut-Ins. I kept saying all this absolutely bizarre stuff I guess like: *I want to know you I want to know everything about you.* Then. She told me on the drive back that she was a pathological liar so all of this stuff she told me about her whole life and family and everything was just made up. Maybe the stuff she'd said to me about what she'd. All of it, I guess. And it didn't matter at all because...it had nothing to do with her.

HARRIET. What did it have to do with?

MEG. Becoming good at experiencing pleasure. And.

HARRIET. / Oh.

MEG. Thinking: Dude why are you so busy doing convenient things.

HARRIET. Did you ever see her again?

MEG. No.

HARRIET. What will you do if you quit your job?

> *(**MEG** sighs. Pours more wine, smiles at **HARRIET.**)*

MEG. Don't know. Maybe we should go hop trains and find seasonal work somewhere.

MATILDA. *Well* I think I have to *go*! Leslie – my daughter is Leslie – she's sick. She has this awful poop virus and I feel bad leaving Arthur to it. I'm late, as usual, already late.

> *(She grabs a drink, maybe not her own, and finishes it quickly.)*

HARRIET. No! Don't leave. It's early. Have another beer. We can talk about you.

> *(Somewhere nearby, a police siren gets loud for a moment –)*

> *(**MATILDA** breaks out in song – a memory of playing Annie Oakley in the 1971 senior year production at Rosati-Kain High School. In the middle of her song, the police siren grows faint, then silent.)*

MATILDA.

> BEHIND THE HILL, THERE'S A BUSY LITTLE STILL
> WHERE YOUR PAPPY'S WORKIN' IN THE MOONLIGHT.
> YOUR LOVIN' PA ISN'T QUITE WITHIN THE LAW,
> SO HE'S HIDIN' THERE BEHIND THE HILL.
> BYE, BYE, BABY.
> STOP YER YAWNIN'.
> DON'T CRY, BABY.
> DAY WILL BE DAWNIN'.
> AND WHEN IT DOES, FROM THE MOUNTAIN WHERE HE WAS,
> HE'LL BE COMIN' WITH A JUG OF MOONSHINE.
> SO COUNT YER SHEEEEEEEEEEEEP
> MAMA'S SINGIN' YOU TO SLEEP –
> WITH A MOONSHINE LULLABY.

> *(**HARRIET** and **MEG** stare at **MATILDA**.)*

MEG. That was really good.

MATILDA. All right. Bye.

HARRIET. Will you ask again about the car when you get home?

MATILDA. Sure.

HARRIET. *Sure?* Do you not want to go?

MATILDA. It's irresponsible.

HARRIET. *(Devastated.)* What?

MATILDA. I have a sick kid who's pooping everywhere. You've already accused me of neglect.

HARRIET. *I* didn't accuse you. I said you would *be accused.* I think you should stay here, stay the night.

MATILDA. I can't.

HARRIET. You don't want to.

MATILDA. I can't. It's getting dark anyway.

    (It is getting dark.)

HARRIET. We'll get the stuff out!

MEG. It's my first night at the Serious Women's / Club –!

MATILDA. Two Serious / Ladies.

HARRIET. One more beer!

MATILDA. Ugh I can't say no to you.

HARRIET. Yes you can.

MATILDA. No I can't.

HARRIET. Yes you can.

MATILDA. How? When?

HARRIET. Just. Constantly.

MATILDA. Fine but not right now. I'm saying yes, but – but not for long, really. I have / to get –

HARRIET. I know! I know.

MATILDA. I want to hear the rest about this motorcycle – this *object* you "discovered" but – / then I'll have to

HARRIET. All right! I know. It's all right; it's all right.

    (She runs downstairs. **MATILDA** *stares at* **MEG.***)*

MATILDA. Oh, I have to help her get the –

    (She runs downstairs.)

    *(***MEG** *pours herself more wine.)*

(She's getting a little cold. She puts her button-up back on over her thrash metal t-shirt. She turns on the radio, then hits play on the cassette controls. There is a static-y crunching sound. **MEG** *squints, turns the volume way up: What is it?)*

*(***HARRIET*** *resurfaces, dragging an extension chord as far as it will reach.* **MATILDA** *follows her with a lamp.)*

MEG. What is this?

HARRIET. *That* is Matilda.

MEG. Doing what.

MATILDA. Art.

HARRIET. Luke left his old voice recorder here. Matilda stole it.

MATILDA. You gave it to me.

HARRIET. Sure.

MATILDA. I make you beautiful works of art.

HARRIET. Meg, what do you think? Do you like / this?

MEG. What is it? What is the –

HARRIET. It's Matilda. Chewing.

*(***MATILDA*** *thinks this is hilarious.)*

MATILDA. This one's a carrot.

HARRIET. Crunching. She tape-records herself eating crunchy food and then sneaks the tape in there when I'm not looking.

MATILDA. You can sell those for a million dollars when I'm dead!

HARRIET. These aren't as charming as you think they are.

MATILDA. I bet you listen to them when you fall asleep at night.

HARRIET. I – no! I. I'm going to burn them.

(They go back downstairs. MEG *turns off the tape.)*

(The radio plays?*)

(MEG *gets the binoculars, looks out –)*

(MATILDA *brings up another lamp [or five, or an electric menorah, or Christmas tree lights].)*

(HARRIET *comes out of the window with two beers. She hands one to* **MEG**. **MEG** *declines,* **HARRIET** *holds both –)*

(MEG *keeps her gaze out through the binoculars.)*

HARRIET. *(Re: binoculars.)* Is something happening?

MEG. Something's about to.

HARRIET. What.

MEG. Teenagers. One is thinking about...ohhh?

HARRIET. Teenagers?

MEG. They're really young.

    (Quiet. MEG *watches a moment.)*

HARRIET. What are they doing?

MEG. The one just took the other's shirt off. Now she's. They're feeling each other up. Oh. She's going for... She's putting her hand down his pants.
You wanna see?

HARRIET. Yes.

MEG. Okay.

    (She gives **HARRIET** *the binoculars.)*

    (She moves **HARRIET***'s body toward where she was looking – stands extremely close –)*

HARRIET. Oh. Where.

---

*A license to produce *Dr. Ride's American Beach House* does not include a performance license for any third-party or copyrighted music. Licensees should create an original composition or use music in the public domain. For further information, please see Music Use Note on page 3.

MEG. Right there.

HARRIET. Where.

MEG. Just kidding nothing's happening. You really wanted to watch those teenagers though.

HARRIET. Of course I did.

(**MEG** *takes the binoculars back.*)

MEG. Nothing going on at all.

(**MATILDA** *has brought up the rest of the stuff.* **HARRIET** *hands her the beer she'd brought for* **MEG** *–*)

(*Then, suddenly, they all look at the radio –*)

(*Maybe* **HARRIET** *turns it up.*)

(*It gets very, very dark.*)

MALE VOICE 1. Earlier today, reporters talked to Sally Ride's mother, Joyce Ride, who is in Cape Canaveral with several of Sally's friends to attend tomorrow's launch. Joyce Ride described her daughter as "obsessively private." She told reporters that she was surprised that Sally was smiling with excitement as she went into quarantine before the morning liftoff. Joyce Ride did not expect her daughter to be able to be so quote pleasant about the media attention, and said that Sally had found the press to be the most difficult part of her astronaut training. Sally's sister, Reverend Karen Scott, described Sally as a quote grown-up tomboy, and was impressed with her public face as she got ready for NASA's seventh space shuttle mission. This mission – STS-7 – would be nearly routine by now if it weren't for the presence of Sally Ride, who will of course, be the first American woman in space. We're at t-minus ten hours now. More later from Cape Canaveral.

MALE VOICE 2. Oh yes.

(*A soda can pops open –*)

Oh yes. It's Vess.

MALE VOICES.

> *Take me out to the ball game,*
> *Take me out to the crowd,*
> *buy me some peanuts and Cracker Jacks –*

MALE VOICE 2. It's what Ozzie flips over.

MALE VOICES.

> *Cuz it's root-root-root for the Cardinals,*
> *if they don't win it's a shame.*

MALE VOICE 2. You'll flip, too.

> *(The sound of someone taking a sip of Vess.)*

It's the bubbly taste you love...for less! It's Vess.

MALE VOICES.

> *For it's one, two, three strikes you're out –*
> *at the old ball game!*

> *(An electronic instrumental version of an American patriotic song – something repetitive and upbeat.*)*

MALE VOICE 1. Thanks for listening to KHTR HitRadio 103 St. Louis. You're stuck with me, the station nerd, so tonight we are tuned into the STS-7 space mission, set to launch tomorrow, Saturday June eighteenth, at seven thirty-three a.m. The countdown at the Kennedy Space Center has begun. The shuttle will deploy two communications satellites, one for Canada, and one for Indonesia. There will be other experiments onboard, including a study of how zero gravity affects the social behaviors of an ant colony. Miss Ride won't be the only lady making news aboard the Challenger. She'll have to make room for Norma, the ant colony queen.

HARRIET. *(To MATILDA.)* / Norma, the ant queen.

---

*A license to produce *Dr. Ride's American Beach House* does not include a performance license for any third-party or copyrighted music. Licensees should create an original composition or use music in the public domain. For further information, please see Music Use Note on page 3.

MALE VOICE 1. We'll have Grant Carson on later, a former NASA employee, and he'll answer any listener questions. For now, relax, and enjoy this summer night tune – just for you. This is W-ROZ.

> *(It's completely dark outside. A melancholic pop tune plays.*)
>
> *(They listen for just a moment –)*
>
> *(**HARRIET** reaches for a cigarette.)*
>
> *(She realizes they're gone –)*
>
> *(**MEG** looks out through the binoculars. **MATILDA** starts to find a harmony with the song, struggles, then –)*
>
> *(The phone rings.)*

HARRIET. Is that the phone?

> *(They all listen. It rings.)*

It's my – it's Luke.

MATILDA. You'd better answer it, but not / too much.

HARRIET. I'm going! I'm –

MATILDA. But don't take too *long* I mean. I've got to go.

HARRIET. You've "got" to / nothing.

MATILDA. Go! Go!

HARRIET. I'm going!

> *(She disappears down the stairs.)*

(Offstage.) Don't put any vegetable cassettes in there.

> *(Maybe **MEG** keeps looking through the binoculars.)*

MEG. Thanks for inviting me over.

MATILDA. I think Two Serious Ladies Book Club is doomed.

---

*A license to produce *Dr. Ride's American Beach House* does not include a performance license for any third-party or copyrighted music. Licensees should create an original composition or use music in the public domain. For further information, please see Music Use Note on page 3.

MEG. Maybe we should read a book.

MATILDA. We did once and it was a disaster.

MEG. The book?

MATILDA. The talking about it. We should read things in different years and never mention them.

MEG. I have two ideas for books we could read.

MATILDA. No thanks.

MEG. Could I see your poems?

MATILDA. No.

MEG. Do you still write?

(**MATILDA** *nods.*)

MATILDA. No.

MEG. What did you write about?

(**MATILDA** *shrugs.*)

MATILDA. The poem that got me into graduate school was about playing Annie Oakley but they thought it was about Vietnam.

MEG. What does Harriet write about.

MATILDA. Body parts but not sexually.

MEG. I want to read some.

MATILDA. You should read Harriet's and tell her they're good.

MEG. Aren't they?

MATILDA. Yes. It's always been annoying.

MEG. Have you two...

(*She smiles, unsure of herself?*)

MATILDA. What.

MEG. Are you – do you have – have you had...physical... sex? Or is this all more of an abstract kind of.

MATILDA. Kind of what.

MEG. Never mind. It's not my business, sorry. It's not my –

MATILDA. It's fine.

(*Maybe* **MEG** *waits a moment for* **MATILDA** *to go on –*)

MEG. Well, anyway – books. I'll. Maybe I'll start my own... club. And I'll...

MATILDA. Sorry about the night. About the club.

MEG. Don't be.

MATILDA. You wanted us to be more –

MEG. I don't know what I wanted except to drink this wine and to not be.

MATILDA. At a bar.

MEG. At home with myself.

MATILDA. Are you emotionally unstable would you say?

MEG. Oh are you used to more stable emotions?

(Tiny still. This is funny?)

It's just I imagined you met me and thought...oh... that dude can be in a book club. And I thought: wow. Maybe like: that's a more interesting...

*(**HARRIET** resurfaces.)*

MATILDA. What.

HARRIET. My mom died.

MEG. Oh my god.

HARRIET. It's okay.

(Quiet.)

The person who called me – my – said *Mom passed* and for some reason I thought *what a stupid thing to say.*

(Quiet.)

MEG. Do you want me to leave?

HARRIET. I'm fine. My mother was in a lot of pain. I didn't think I cared about her one way or the other, but I. Anyway that's why I was in Florida last weekend. Now she's dead.

(Quiet.)

*(**HARRIET** takes another beer, pulls out the pack of cigarettes – they're gone –)*

(She shrugs.)

HARRIET. Weird.

> (*She picks up the binoculars.* **MATILDA** *and*
> **MEG** *stare at her. She looks at something as*
> *she speaks.*)

She's – from the phone – she's my half-sister, I guess.

MATILDA. What.

HARRIET. Why did I do that? I don't know why I went there? She might as well have been an uninspiring second grade teacher or. But I guess it's only: well do you want to see your mother before she dies or do you not?

> (*Shrugs.*)

I didn't realize how *upset* I'd – I was staying at the hospice – her. I didn't have any place else to stay. So I sleep on the couch in her room, mostly. And these people who live there, who live down in Florida, they come to see her, her *other kids*, and they have weird hair and clothes and sound different from anyone I've ever met.

MATILDA. Woah / they're related to you.

HARRIET. They're wearing jewelry and one has a baby, which means I'm a. They bring photographs and they say *there's Mom at the pool in Madeira.* And I think oh, that's fucking nice, there you are swimming with *my* goddamn mother. Meanwhile, I'm somewhere – with a –. These photographs! They're showing me all of these photographs. She's at the park with *children*, my mother. The zoo. My mother, the beach. My mother, standing in front of somebody's – I don't know – brand-new *Ford.* She can't send me a postcard for thirty-one years but she's holding babies and washing dishes and making someone's birthday dinner and I'm. I show up and I'm her *fucking* daughter standing there while all of these people talk about this entire *life* they have with her. What must they think of me? I was just left somewhere else and no one ever heard from me or about me or if they did maybe they thought it was because I was some awful – what must they think? I don't even like her but I want to grab her – all emaciated, blue – and make her, make her into my mom – put her in someone's car and photograph myself with her in different locations just so I can sit there with them and say here *we* are at the...gas station, here *we* are at a highway sign...all these... *I* remember her too, *I* remember her too. They get these *memories* with my mom – I! And meanwhile I'm I'm I'm not –. I'm no one.

(*Quiet.*)

MEG. I'll be right back.

(**MATILDA** *and* **HARRIET** *don't look at* **MEG**. *She disappears down the stairs.*)

HARRIET. I thought I was going to get some money. I spent everything flying down there.

MATILDA. I know.

HARRIET. I didn't. She left me the house.

MATILDA. / Oh.

HARRIET. I have to pay taxes on it. I can't afford it.

MATILDA. That person on the phone told you that?

HARRIET. She said *Mom left you the house.* I said *oh. Um.* She said you can keep it or sell it but someone does have to pay the taxes on it in the meantime. I don't have / *anything.*

MATILDA. Yeah.

HARRIET. Mm-hm. Do you want to move there with me?

MATILDA. No.

(*Still.*)

(*Re:* **MEG**.) What do you think she's getting?

HARRIET. She probably left.

MATILDA. She didn't.

(*Still. Did she?* **HARRIET** *turns cold.*)

HARRIET. It's not a big deal. You can go home.

MATILDA. Well not this *second*, I. Why would I leave this second?

(**HARRIET** *shrugs.*)

HARRIET. If you want to then you should. None of this is a big deal.

(**MEG** *comes back up, holding a cassette.*)

MEG. I had to cue it up really quick. Maybe this isn't like – what you usually listen to, but.

(*She puts the cassette in the boombox.*)

I'm going to turn this way up.

(*She hits play and turns it way up.*)

(*The tape is cued to a song – some sort of early metal.* [*It doesn't sound like anything they've ever heard.*])

(*They stand and listen.*)

(**MEG** *gets into it somehow.*)

(*Maybe* **HARRIET** *does.*)

(*Maybe, eventually,* **MATILDA** *does.*)

(*Suddenly* **NORMA** *appears at the top of the stairs. She holds an aerosol can of Raid.*)

(**MEG** *rushes to click stop on the cassette.*)

Sorry. Sorry it was so loud.

NORMA. Who's that?

MEG. / I'm Meg.

HARRIET. Meg. Our friend Meg.

(**NORMA** *frowns.*)

(*She sees a flying insect. She holds the can of Raid up and tries to spray it directly, though*)

---

*A license to produce *Dr. Ride's American Beach House* does not include a performance license for any third-party or copyrighted music. Licensees should create an original composition or use music in the public domain. For further information, please see Music Use Note on page 3.

this motion takes her over ten seconds, and whatever she had spotted is certainly out of reach. A puff of toxic mist.)

NORMA. I don't care about the. Music. There are flies in the.

HARRIET. I saw them.

NORMA. House. What?

HARRIET. I've seen the flies.

NORMA. Well. Now: there are flies getting in. Maybe you'll remember not to open and close the window so. Much.

HARRIET. They're always there.

> *(**NORMA** points to **HARRIET**'s cigarettes.)*
>
> *(**HARRIET** reaches for the pack, realizes it's empty.)*

Oh. They're gone.

NORMA. Ah. Well. Glad enough to know you're up here –

> *(She tries to shake her hips.)*

So good for you.

HARRIET. Yes. We were just thinking.

NORMA. What?

HARRIET. *Thinking.*

NORMA. About what?

HARRIET. About my mother.

NORMA. That's nice.

HARRIET. Yep!

NORMA. Well when you're through with. That. Maybe you can move the window unit.

HARRIET. Okay. We'll move it soon.

NORMA. Good. Ah. Well.

HARRIET. In a few minutes.

NORMA. Now: I've gone ahead and decided. I'm gonna call them. I, now, the last thing I want is to be a bother, but I can't help. I'm gonna go ahead and call them to come take care of the gosh d'ed flies. I don't need to keep a nice or upscale kind of place but I do need to maintain a place where I trust a fly won't be in my. Soup. Oh they hate me over at the exterminators, at the. At the. Every place. Oh they hate me calling. I'm sure they think –

(She waves her hand around.)

Nobody likes me. Not even my sister, and she's supposed. To. But. Now: if you could remember to stop opening and closing the window so much. That would be better. Maybe you will remember to. Not do that. At a certain point you have to think: well nobody likes you. What can you do about it? You have to choose the things you care about. Now: I care about safety. And I care about money. You know. / That.

HARRIET. I know. I like that about you.

NORMA. You what?

HARRIET. I said I *like that* about you.

NORMA. Thank you. Anyway. Lucille's still down there. She's going like this.

(She imitates someone clumsily swatting at flies.)

I'm sure she's thinking: what kind of a place is this? My ex-friend Rosa used to have us over for –. Anyway, Lucille's the one with the car, so if she wants to just leave, well then? I told her: you come over here, you eat all my food, you complain to me. I'm just trying to get a thing or two. Accomplished. I've got a whole music and poem collection to worry –. And here we are yack-yacking at each other, wasting electricity. But now: she's watching the news and waving at flies and thinking I haven't done a good. Job. I can tell. And the news is bad.

HARRIET. You don't like that they're going to space.

NORMA. Where are they going?

HARRIET. I said: You don't like that they're going to *space*, Dr. Sally Ride and all of them. And, oh, oh: they're going with / an ant named Norma –

NORMA. Well I don't know about. No one's talking about *that*. Right now they're telling terrible stories about the biggest flood somewhere out west, maybe in all history. All this stuff getting. Stomped. And this. Massacre. In Lebanon for two days, people dead all over from. Since we helped the Israel-ese out of there, troops out'a. Bombs all over. And and in New York, some poor kid dies of this immune system deficiency and they've quarantined his friend and now: we're all a bunch of helpless scums is what *we* are. I can't stand it. And my sister down there swatting flies to remind me that I'm. A failure: now that isn't helping. But good for Sally Ride.

HARRIET. Want a beer?

NORMA. No. Now don't forget to close this window. Maybe your friend is leaving it open.

MEG. Nice / meeting you!

>(**NORMA** *leaves.*)

>(**HARRIET** *calls after her:*)

HARRIET. I don't think there's anything we can do about the flies.

>(*She stares at* **MATILDA** *a moment.*)

I stared at the NASA beach house in the dark for a long time like I was out of my mind or...as – I thought if I looked at it long enough my – I could affect it. But we left. We drove back – we drove back to his house. It took so long and it started getting light out and everything looked different. It looked like we were in a refrigerator. Bugs got in my eyes. I was disgusting. Then it got bright and I was sweating when we finally finally got to his driveway and I said *could I see your marble collection?* Oh – I asked him if I could see his marble collection. And he was so happy. He couldn't believe his luck.

He kept all of his marbles in these flat boxes. They were beautiful. I said to him *these are beautiful.* And he said *these are the rare ones.* They were clear and they had little *figures* inside. They were a bit stupid, but some were nice. They were glass or something with tiny animals inside of them. There was a tiny fawn and a tiny turtle. A lamb. A pigeon. So many of them – and he said – I assume he was telling me the truth – he said he had seven thousand dollars' worth of that kind of – oh! Sulphate. Sulphite. Sulphide marbles. They're very difficult to make he said. I didn't ask but he told me. He said they were very difficult to make because even if you have only a tiny little – a slip of – however it is you make them – even if you make the tiniest mistake, air bubbles get inside the marble and they distort the figure. The idea is to be able to see the little animal inside.

He asked me if I wanted one of the fancy marbles, and I said, *yes I do want one.* And he said he would give me this one with a little lizard inside of it. I told him that instead of the lizard marble I liked this marble with a crow.

MEG. That's a poem that's a poetry thing / or?

HARRIET. No. I have no idea why I liked the crow one. And he said I could have it for seventy-five dollars and I said *oh I thought you were just giving it to me* and then he felt bad but not so bad. He said *no, but that's a good deal.* And I said *I don't have seventy-five dollars.* The word *crow* started getting to me. I said it in all these accents. I said craw, croo. *(Bad German accent.) The one with the crow.* Then I got nervous he didn't like me anymore, which – ordinarily wouldn't have mattered but I was concerned it would take away my power.

MEG. Why do you think you wanted power?

HARRIET. It was nice, having all that power. So I said *never mind.* I said *I don't really need a marble.* I said *will you let me drive your motorcycle* and he laughed because he thought I was kidding.

MEG. Do you know how to drive a motorcycle?

HARRIET. How hard could it be? He can drive it. Sally Dr. Ride can drive a space shuttle. How hard can it be? But he said *no I am sorry you cannot drive the motorcycle,* which – in a way I understood because he probably wanted us both to live. And then he said I could drive his Honda CRX. I said *all right.* So we get into the car and he tells me how to get to the hospice center – but he doesn't say anything – only –

(*She gestures – pointing left and right.*)

And then eventually he says *are you hungry* and I say yes. But then I drive by a restaurant, and look at him, and think about going inside there, and I think: *no.*

And I said: *maybe I don't want anything at all.*

MATILDA. Then what.

HARRIET. Nothing.

(*She shrugs. The phone rings.*)

(*She doesn't move –*)

MATILDA. Don't you want to talk to Luke?

(**HARRIET** *shakes her head.*)

HARRIET. I need a ride.

MATILDA. What – now? / Where?

HARRIET. Yes. Florida.

MATILDA. What are you going to do in Florida right now?

HARRIET. Go to my mother's funeral. Go see her house. My house. Maybe not come back.

MATILDA. Of course you'll come back.

HARRIET. Let's drive down. Let's drive / Arthur's car down.

MATILDA. Not *now.* Not – no. Not yet.

HARRIET. Why not?

MATILDA. Wait. A few days.

(*The phone stops ringing.*)

(*Long quiet.*)

MEG. I would drive you now. Only I.

HARRIET. You want to?

MEG. I drank too much.

HARRIET. I could drive.

>　*(Still.)*

MEG. We could go in the morning, if you want.

HARRIET. / Yes.

MATILDA. No.

MEG. We can take a trip.

>　*(**HARRIET** nods.)*

HARRIET. You can stay here, sleep here / tonight if –

MATILDA. What's wrong with you?

HARRIET. What? It doesn't have –

MATILDA. It's / insane.

HARRIET. It doesn't have to do with you.

>　*(The phone rings again –)*

>　*(**HARRIET** doesn't move to get it.)*

MATILDA. Talk to Luke.

HARRIET. No.

>　*(The phone rings.)*

　　I'll drive.

MEG. Maybe.

HARRIET. You'll stay here?

MEG. Sure.

HARRIET. I want to hear the countdown.

MEG. All right.

HARRIET. We'll go right after them.

MEG. We can go at the same time they do.

HARRIET. Or... Okay. We'll go at the same time / as them.

MATILDA. What if / you...

HARRIET. What?

MATILDA. I think this is a strange and. A bad idea.

HARRIET. Okay. *(To* **MEG.***)* They leave at 6:33. If you want to listen.

MEG. Sure.

HARRIET. And then we can go.

> *(***MEG*** nods.)*

If you still feel like it.

MEG. Could be fun.

MATILDA. It won't / be fun.

HARRIET. Oh I don't have any money for gas.

MEG. It's all right.

MATILDA. What are you going to do about work on Sunday?

HARRIET. I'm not going to be there.

MATILDA. I don't understand what you're doing.

HARRIET. It's okay.

MATILDA. Maybe I can get the car in a few days – maybe / we, in a few –

HARRIET. It's okay. You can't go, it's. Fine.

> *(***HARRIET*** and* **MATILDA*** are suddenly illuminated oddly – colorful, eerie – [Or maybe it's dark, almost too dark to see them. Or maybe it's bright – it becomes too bright?])*

> **The sky is different; the river is the Atlantic Ocean. The highway is gone. This is the NASA Beach House.**

> *(***HARRIET*** is somehow* **SALLY RIDE,*** and* **MATILDA*** is somehow* **MOLLY TYSON,*** upon a surprise arrival at the Beach House –)*

> *(Their voices are amplified.)*

MOLLY TYSON. Sally.

SALLY RIDE. Molly?

MOLLY TYSON. Are you surprised?

SALLY RIDE. I'm surprised they let you in.

MOLLY TYSON. Jack Abbey invited me.

SALLY RIDE. Why?

MOLLY TYSON. Pretend you're happier.

SALLY RIDE. I'm happy. I'm happy.

MOLLY TYSON. He said you were nervous.

SALLY RIDE. Not more nervous than anyone else.

MOLLY TYSON. Good.

SALLY RIDE. He invited you here because he thinks I'm nervous?

MOLLY TYSON. He said you were nervous. I'm glad he / called me and not –

SALLY RIDE. He's watching us from up there.

MOLLY TYSON. Who where?

SALLY RIDE. Inside, in the kitchen, Jack Abbey is watching us.

> *(They wave.)*

MOLLY TYSON. Where's Mr. Hawley?

SALLY RIDE. At home.

MOLLY TYSON. I thought I might get lucky and get to say hi how are you and / all – that whole thing.

SALLY RIDE. I know you love – I know.

MOLLY TYSON. You don't look nervous to me but that doesn't mean a lot.

SALLY RIDE. What about you? Are you nervous?

MOLLY TYSON. Don't ask me that; I'm here to comfort you.

SALLY RIDE. I think you're really nervous.

> *(**MOLLY TYSON** nods.)*

MOLLY TYSON. But then I – yes. I am, but then I think: it's you. It's you. You're only going to make things go perfectly well. I don't have a clue what you'll do up there, but you'll be perfect. You'll make it go perfectly well.

SALLY RIDE. Yeah.

MOLLY TYSON. You know that.

SALLY RIDE. Yeah.

> *(She probably does?)*

Do you remember when we were juniors and we had the division finals at Chapel Hill?

MOLLY TYSON. Yes.

SALLY RIDE. And we had the party after, with that other women's team / at that terrible basement place –

MOLLY TYSON. Yes. That party. Yes. I – yes. I will never forget that – that / party.

SALLY RIDE. And I said: I don't remember what I said but – / we left.

MOLLY TYSON. You asked if I wanted to leave.

> *(Maybe* **SALLY RIDE** *is impressed with herself.)*

SALLY RIDE. Yes.

MOLLY TYSON. You said: Do you want to leave with me?

SALLY RIDE. That's what I said?

MOLLY TYSON. Yes.

SALLY RIDE. That was a time I was really nervous.

MOLLY TYSON. You didn't seem nervous.

SALLY RIDE. I was.

> *(Quiet.)*

MOLLY TYSON. I told all the kids at my tennis camp that I know you.

SALLY RIDE. Mm-hm.

MOLLY TYSON. They are very impressed with me. I told them I showed them the Time Magazine article about how I taught you Shakespeare.

SALLY RIDE. It doesn't say that.

MOLLY TYSON. It nearly says that. It's very flattering.

SALLY RIDE. I'm glad.

MOLLY TYSON. They're very impressed with me. Well – they're more impressed with you of course but – I – but I like that too.

> *(***SALLY RIDE*** *nods.)*

(Wait – now does she seem a little nervous?)

MOLLY TYSON. You're going to be great.

    *(**SALLY RIDE** nods.)*

Have you eaten? Can you have a glass of wine or something?

SALLY RIDE. No. / Yes, I had –

MOLLY TYSON. I / know.

SALLY RIDE. I barbecued.

MOLLY TYSON. I want to document this.

    (A camera. She turns on the flash.)

SALLY RIDE. No.

MOLLY TYSON. I thought it would be swankier here.

SALLY RIDE. I don't think the beach house is the primary concern.

MOLLY TYSON. I didn't mean to insult NASA, your / only true –

SALLY RIDE. It's not – I'm not / insulted.

MOLLY TYSON. Your only true love.

    (She snaps a picture. Flash.)

No...

SALLY RIDE. What do you want me to do?

MOLLY TYSON. I want you to smile like you really know me.

SALLY RIDE. I do really know you.

MOLLY TYSON. I want this to be a once-in-a-lifetime moment that I capture just for myself so I need you to look how you really look.

SALLY RIDE. How do I really look?

MOLLY TYSON. I'm not sure try smiling differently.

    (Flash.)

Mm. Okay don't smile.

    *(**SALLY RIDE** does something else.)*

No. Never mind, smile how you were smiling before.

(Flash.)

Not quite what I was after but it will do. It's / good.

SALLY RIDE. Good.

MOLLY TYSON. It's good enough.

SALLY RIDE. I want you to stay.

MOLLY TYSON. With you? Do I get to come along on the shuttle?

SALLY RIDE. For the night.

MOLLY TYSON. Mm-hm?

SALLY RIDE. You miss me?

(**MOLLY TYSON** *nods.*)

Don't go home.

MOLLY TYSON. I'm staying at the hotel / with –

(Music?)*

SALLY RIDE. I know. I. Good. You can't sleep here anyway.

MOLLY TYSON. No?

SALLY RIDE. No – they'd. They wouldn't. And Jack's –

(They look up.)

(**MOLLY TYSON** *waves inside.*)

(Music –)*

I'm glad we can say goodbye.

(**MOLLY TYSON** *nods.*)

MOLLY TYSON. Yeah.

SALLY RIDE. Are you hungry?

MOLLY TYSON. I'm okay.

(They notice – they love this song –)

(Is it the same song Matilda sang at the beginning?)

---

*A license to produce Dr. Ride's American Beach House does not include a performance license for any third-party or copyrighted music. Licensees should create an original composition or use music in the public domain. For further information, please see Music Use Note on page 3.

(Somehow, they get close to each other.)

(They dance.)

(It's a painfully short moment before – the world changes.)

(The song is suddenly coming from the radio.)

(Are they on the roof or at the beach house?)

(**HARRIET** [**SALLY RIDE**] *leaves –)*

(**MATILDA** *is alone.)*

(She listens for just a moment.)

(Dark.)

End of Play